The Boxcar Children® Mysteries

THE FINDERS KEEPERS MYSTERY

created by
GERTRUDE CHANDLER WARNER

Illustrated by Hodges Soileau

ALBERT WHITMAN & Company
Morton Grove, Illinois

The Finders Keepers Mystery
created by Gertrude Chandler Warner;
illustrated by Hodges Soileau.

ISBN 0-8075-5548-7(hardcover)
ISBN 0-8075-5549-5(paperback)

Cover art by David Cunningham.

For more information about Albert Whitman & Company,
visit our web site at www.albertwhitman.com.

Contents

CHAPTER 1

The Haunted Shortcut

"It's almost time for dinner, Benny. We have to hurry," Jessie Alden told her six-year-old brother. They were walking home from the post office, where they had bought stamps for their grandfather, James Alden, and mailed a letter for their house-keeper, Mrs. McGregor.

Benny was picking something up off the sidewalk. "Look at this rock. It has sparkles in it," he said. "Maybe it has a diamond hidden inside."

"I'm pretty sure it doesn't," said Jessie, who was twelve. "Come on."

"How do you know?" Benny asked.

"Because diamonds come from diamond mines a long, long way from here," Jessie said, smiling.

"Oh," said Benny, disappointed. He slipped the rock in his pocket just in case Jessie was wrong. He fell into step beside his sister and walked quickly along with her for almost a block. His steps slowed, though, as she turned at the corner of the next street. "Hey!" he said. "This is the wrong way!"

"Not if we take the shortcut," Jessie told him.

Stopping, Benny said nervously, "The shortcut?"

"Through the backyard of the old Bidwell house and then along the path," said Jessie. "You know, it comes out right on our street."

"No!" cried Benny. "That old house is haunted!"

"It's not haunted, Benny. It's just an old

house that no one lives in," Jessie said. "Hurry up."

Benny stayed where he was. "That house is haunted," he repeated stubbornly.

"There's no such thing as a haunted house, Benny. You know that. Besides, we're not going *in* the house, we're going around it," Jessie argued.

Benny didn't move.

"Henry and Violet and Watch are probably already home," Jessie said. "Maybe they're eating dinner. Or maybe they've finished and they're eating all the dessert."

"They're not home yet," Benny said. But he began to walk slowly after Jessie. "They went to the grocery store, and it takes lots longer to go to the grocery store than the post office. And Henry and Violet wouldn't eat all the dessert."

"Watch would," Jessie teased.

Henry was the oldest of the four Alden children. He was fourteen. Violet was ten. No one knew how old Watch was. He was a smart, brave little dog that the children had found when they lived alone in an old boxcar in the woods. The Aldens were orphans, and they didn't know that they had such a kind grandfather who was looking for them.

But Grandfather found them, and now they all lived together in his big white house in Greenfield. Grandfather had the old boxcar brought to the backyard so the four children and Watch could play in it whenever they wanted.

Benny smiled a little, picturing Watch eating everyone's dessert.

Jessie added, "Mrs. McGregor said something about brownies, I think. Maybe she put vanilla ice cream on her grocery list."

Benny walked a little faster. He liked dessert, especially Mrs. McGregor's special brownies. "Okay," he said. "We can take the shortcut. But we have to run fast."

"We will," Jessie promised.

The old Bidwell house was the last one on a dead-end street. Shutters with missing and broken slats were closed over all the downstairs windows. Vines and climbing roses grew everywhere. The house was surrounded by trees with low-hanging branches that made the old place look even gloomier.

Jessie stopped in front of the rusty fence. She took a deep breath, then stepped between two bent iron railings, into the yard. She reached back to help Benny through.

"I don't know if this is a good idea," said Benny.

"Come on, Benny," Jessie said. "It's just an empty old house, that's all."

"It's getting dark," said Benny.

"The longer we stand here, the darker it will get," Jessie said.

"I know," said Benny unhappily. He squeezed through the two iron railings. He stood up and moved very close to Jessie.

"I'll lead the way," Jessie said.

"Go fast," Benny told her.

"I will," she said. "Let's go!" Jessie sprinted forward. She jumped over a tree branch, and Benny jumped, too. She dodged around a big rock, and Benny dodged, too.

Weeds slapped their legs. Leaves scurried out from underfoot as if they were alive.

Benny wanted to close his eyes, but he was afraid he would fall. If he fell, something might come out of the house and get him.

Benny tried not to look at the house, but he couldn't help it. He kept glancing back at it as they ran. Was that a broom he saw in the corner of the porch? Did ghosts sweep porches?

"Jessie," Benny croaked breathlessly.

But Jessie didn't hear him. She'd slowed down to pick her way through a tangle of briars.

Suddenly, one of the shutters banged open. Light flared in the window.

"Jessie!" shrieked Benny. "It's the ghost!"

He ran past his sister, barely noticing the briars that grabbed at his ankles. Jessie spun around and almost fell. "Benny, wait!"

Benny kept running. He ran as fast as he'd ever run in his life. He could hear Jessie's footsteps close behind him as he sprinted for home.

Benny reached the front path just as Henry and Violet were carrying the groceries into the house. Watch saw Benny first and bounded toward him, barking and wagging his tail.

Jessie was right behind Benny. "Benny, w-wait," she gasped.

"What's wrong?" asked Henry.

"Are you all right?" Violet asked.

Benny stopped running and bent over to catch his breath. He glanced up at the neatly painted shutters on the windows of their house and the warm glow of friendly light from the kitchen.

"Now I am," he said. He took a deep breath.

"You look as if you'd seen a ghost," Violet joked. She smiled, not so worried now that she saw Benny and Jessie were both unhurt.

Benny's answer made her smile disappear. "We did," he said. "We did see a ghost."

CHAPTER 2

Treasure in the Attic

"What?" said Henry. He looked at Jessie. "You saw a ghost?"

Jessie shook her head. "I don't know what Benny saw," she said. "We took the short-cut past the old Bidwell house. I heard a shutter fall or something, and the next thing I knew, Benny was running so fast I could barely keep up."

The back door opened. Mrs. McGregor peered out. "Dinner is ready and your Grandfather is waiting," she said in her sternest voice — which wasn't very stern at all. In fact, Mrs. McGregor was, as usual, smiling.

For a moment, Benny forgot ghosts. "Brownies?" he asked.

"For dessert," said Mrs. McGregor. "Come in now and give me those groceries and wash your hands."

"And then you can tell us all about the ghost," Henry said.

By the time they'd gotten to dessert, Benny had told his family all about the broom on the porch, the shutter that had banged open, and the ghostly light at the window.

"I've never heard of ghosts who sweep porches," Grandfather said, his eyes twinkling. "But you are very smart to notice all those things, Benny."

Benny wasn't afraid now. He was safe at home and eating dessert with his family. He nodded. "I know," he said. "It's because I'm a good detective."

That made the others laugh.

"It does sound mysterious," Violet said

thoughtfully. She looked at Jessie. "You didn't see anything suspicious or scary?"

Jessie shook her head. "No. I was too busy trying to keep up with Benny." She made a face at her younger brother. He grinned and made a face back.

"Let's go over to the old house tomorrow and take a look," said Henry.

"Go back?" said Benny. His smile disappeared.

"Sure. It'll be daylight, and we'll all go together. We'll take Watch, too," Henry said.

"Don't worry, Benny," Jessie added. "I'm sure there's a simple, logical explanation for what you saw."

"And no ghost," Violet said.

"Okay," Benny said reluctantly. "We'll go tomorrow — but I sure hope you're right."

The next morning, right after breakfast, the four children and Watch walked to the old Bidwell house. This time, they didn't use the shortcut. Benny was careful to let the others go first as they pushed open the rusty gate and headed up the front walk.

"Look," said Henry. He pointed to a battered green van parked in the shadows in the overgrown driveway.

"I guess we didn't notice that last night," Jessie said.

"I don't think a ghost would drive a van, do you?" Violet asked her little brother.

"Probably not," Benny admitted.

"And look," Violet said. "The geraniums in the pots on each side of the front door look as if they've just been planted."

"They have," said a voice.

All of the Aldens jumped, which surprised Watch into giving a quick bark.

"Hi there," said the voice. Henry turned and saw that it belonged to a young woman leaning out of an open window at one end of the porch. The woman's black hair was pulled into a long braid. She had brown eyes and she was smiling. "Are you my new neighbors?" she asked.

"Not exactly," Jessie said. "We live a couple of blocks away. But last night we noticed, well, that something about the house was different, so we came over this morning to check it out."

"Two blocks over is still close enough to be neighbors," declared the woman. "Come on in." Her head disappeared from the window, and a moment later the front door swung open.

"Hi," she said. "I'm Lina Diaz."

"We're the Aldens," said Benny. "Is this your house?"

"It is," said Lina. "I inherited it from my cousin. But he didn't live here — the house has been empty for a long time."

"I know," said Benny.

"Oh," said Violet. She frowned. "But if you're Lina Diaz, why does everyone call this the Bidwell house?"

"Well, it used to be owned by a woman named Hope Bidwell. She was my great-great-aunt," explained Lina. "The house is still full of old-fashioned things. Would you like to come in and take a look?"

"It's not haunted?" asked Benny.

"No!" said Lina. "At least, I'm pretty sure it's not. I spent last night here and didn't see a single ghost." She gave Benny a reassuring smile.

The Aldens followed Lina inside. The open windows let in fresh air and sunshine, but it still looked as if no one had lived in the house for a long time. Everything was dusty. Watch sneezed as he trotted after them.

"It's going to take a lot of work to get this place back in shape," said Lina. "Fortunately, that's one of the things I'm good at. I'm an architect, and it will be fun to work on my own house."

"It's a nice house," Violet said politely. She looked around shyly.

Lina laughed. "It was once," she said, "and it will be again. I've been going through it and labeling things I want to keep and things I don't want. I was just about to take a look in the attic and have some lemonade. Do you want to join me?"

"Yes, please," said Jessie.

"Which do you want to do first? Have lemonade, or look in the attic?" Lina asked.

"The attic," Jessie said at once. The others nodded eagerly.

So Lina led the way up a flight of stairs in the back of the house to a door on a dusty landing. She pushed the door open, and Watch sneezed again. So did Benny and Violet.

"Very dusty, isn't it?" said Lina. She pulled a flashlight from her pocket and used it to find a light switch. A dim light came on. "Oh, dear," Lina said in dismay.

The attic was full of dust — and all kinds of boxes, chairs, tables, lamps, and mysterious, lumpy objects hidden by sheets and blankets. To walk, each of them had to turn sideways to squeeze between piles of furniture and boxes.

Henry said, "I'll go open the curtains on that window over there to let in some more light."

"Good idea," Lina said. "But be careful."

Henry wriggled between two boxes, his feet kicking up dust. A moment later, he'd opened the sagging, faded curtains. Sunlight poured into the attic, and dust swirled from the curtains, thick as smoke. It was Henry's turn to sneeze.

"No one's been in this room for hundreds of years, I think," said Benny. "Like in a fairy tale."

"I don't know about hundreds of years, but it's been a long time," agreed Lina. "There are probably all sorts of great treasures up here."

Benny's eyes lit up. "Pirate treasure?" he said excitedly.

Lina laughed. "I was thinking more of old junk that would be interesting to uncover. But, you know . . ." She trailed off.

"What?" Benny asked.

"Well, people say my Great-great-aunt Hope had a hidden treasure," Lina said casually.

"What do you mean?" asked Violet.

"I mean, she hid something valuable in this house. Nobody knows what it was. It could have been the money she saved for her wedding or a silver tea set that she inherited. Whatever it was, nobody ever found it. The story probably isn't even true."

"A treasure! Let's start looking now!" Benny exclaimed.

"Hold on, Benny," Henry said. He smiled at his younger brother. "We can look for treasure, but we can also help clean the attic."

"That would be just as good as finding treasure, getting all this cleaned up. And then I could have a yard sale," Lina said.

Jessie's eyes sparkled. "A yard sale? We'd love to help!" she said.

"We can get started right away," Violet volunteered.

Lina was surprised. "Are you sure? It's a lot of work."

Henry smiled at her. "That's what neighbors are for."

"Well, okay then," said Lina. "And thanks." She paused and looked around. "Let's have some lemonade and cookies first." She glanced down. "And a bowl of water for Watch. Then we'll go to work on this attic."

The Aldens and Lina worked hard all afternoon. They dusted and swept. They opened and organized boxes full of books and shoes and even old hats. Lina decided that she could use lots of the old furniture, so Henry and Jessie helped her clear out one corner of the attic where she would store it until she needed it.

After just a few hours, they had used up all of Lina's soap and polish. Violet helped make a list of cleaning supplies they would need for the next day. "I'll get poster paper and paint, too, for the yard sale signs," Lina said, making a note on the list.

As he worked, Benny kept an eye out for hidden treasure.

But of all the things they found, nothing seemed to be of much value. Benny was very disappointed.

Just when he was about to give up hope, they uncovered an old cedar trunk in the back corner of the attic.

"A treasure chest!" Benny cried. Lina unhooked the latch and lifted the trunk's heavy lid. A faint odor of cedar reached Benny's nose. He caught a glimpse of faded green silk lining the curved top of the trunk.

"Yes," said Lina. "You could say that."

They all crowded around and peered inside. There in the trunk, as ornate and colorful as a necklace of jewels, was a carefully folded quilt.

"Oh," said Violet in awe. "It's perfect."

Carefully, Lina lifted out the quilt. It was folded in layers of tissue paper, and Violet gathered these up while Jessie and Henry helped Lina spread the quilt over a nearby chair.

"What a beautiful quilt!" said Lina. "It's like something from a museum!"

"Look! More quilts," Benny said, leaning over the trunk's edge.

Lina and the Aldens unfolded five more quilts from the old trunk, each more amazing than the one before. They admired the splashes of color and the tiny, even stitches that held the quilts together.

"Who could have made all these?" Violet wondered aloud.

"My great-great-aunt, Hope Bidwell," said Lina.

"How do you know?" asked Benny.

"Well, my grandfather had a quilt she made, and he always told us about how talented Aunt Hope was at quilting. She sold some of her quilts to make a little extra money when this house was still a farmhouse. The rest she made for the family as gifts for weddings or christenings or birthdays," Lina explained.

"Look at this!" exclaimed Jessie, pointing. In the corner of one of the quilts, the letters HB were embroidered in green. "HB — Hope Bidwell! She signed it with her initials."

"Green was her favorite color, my grandfather said." Lina smiled. "It's mine, too. Apparently, Hope's wedding quilt had lots of green in it."

"Wedding quilt?" said Violet.

"The quilt she made for her marriage. It's sort of a legend in our family, even more than her hidden treasure. Hope was going to marry her true love, you see," Lina explained. "Robert, his name was. After their engagement, Robert went on a trip. While he was gone, Hope sewed a beautiful quilt that they would use when he came home to marry her."

"But he didn't come home," Jessie guessed.

Lina nodded. "Very good, Jessie. No, he didn't come home. The very day Hope finished her wedding quilt, word came that Robert had died of a sudden illness. Hope was overcome with grief. All she had left of him were the letters he'd sent. And nobody ever saw that wedding quilt again."

Violet clasped her hands together. "Oh, what a sad story," she said.

"I know," said Lina. "I was sort of hoping Robert's letters might turn up in the attic. That and her wedding quilt would mean so much to me." She sighed. "But these other quilts are pretty wonderful, too."

"Hey, wait!" Benny said, his voice muf-

fled as he leaned down into the chest.
"There's one more quilt in here!"

Lina rushed over and lifted the last quilt
from the trunk. This quilt wasn't beautiful
like the others. It was made of rough gray
wool, and it didn't have careful, perfect
stitching or embroidery on it as the other
quilts did. It looked as if someone had just
wanted to finish it in a hurry.

"Oh," said Benny, disappointed. "That's
not the wedding quilt. It's not pretty at all.
It doesn't belong with these other quilts."
He dropped his end of the old quilt on a
chair. Lina smoothed the rough fabric and
set the quilt aside.

"Maybe it was just an everyday quilt and
these were special quilts for company," said
Lina. She reached out to touch a velvet
patch on the nearest quilt. "I know these
are special. I wish I could learn more about
them."

"We could look them up at the library,"
said Jessie. "Quilts, I mean."

"And you could call a museum," said Violet. "The State History Museum, maybe?"

"Good ideas," said Lina. "I'll call the museum first thing tomorrow."

"And we'll go to the library as soon as we finish helping you get ready for your yard sale," said Jessie.

"Meanwhile, we should put these quilts back in the trunk," Henry said.

"Yes, to keep them safe," agreed Lina.

The Aldens and Lina carefully folded the quilts and set them back into the trunk. Lina spread the gray everyday quilt on top of the others, then closed the lid.

As they left the attic, Lina glanced back at the cedar trunk. "You know," she said thoughtfully, "when my grandfather told me stories about Great-great-aunt Hope's hidden treasure, I thought it must be gold or silver or jewels. But these quilts are a treasure."

"Yes," said Violet softly. "They are."

CHAPTER 3

Log Cabins and Flying Geese

"Achoo! AAAAAA-CHOOO!" Those were the first sounds the Aldens heard from Edward Munsey. Mr. Munsey was a quilt expert sent by the State History Museum. He had just followed Lina into the attic. The four Aldens had been there all morning helping Lina sort through things for the yard sale.

"It's not as dusty as it was when we first got here," Benny said helpfully.

"Ah, oooh, urgh," said Mr. Munsey, his round face half hidden by a large handkerchief. He whisked the handkerchief away, revealing his watery green eyes. "Allergies," he finally said. He managed to smile. "To dust. Maybe from all the time I've spent in people's attics looking at what they call treasure."

At the mention of treasure, Benny perked up. It was a word he liked. "Lina's grandfather said her great-great-aunt had hidden trea — "

Interrupting quickly, Lina said, "Mr. Munsey, I'd like you to meet my neighbors, Henry, Violet, Benny, and Jessie Alden."

"And Watch," added Benny, pointing toward Watch, who was now curled up in the sunlight from the attic window on a faded pillow. Watch raised his head at the sound of his name — and sneezed, too.

That made the Aldens and Lina laugh.

"I hope you are not allergic to dogs," said Jessie.

"As a matter of fact, and most surprisingly, no," said Mr. Munsey. "Now, am I to look at quilts, or, er, treasure?"

"Quilts," said Lina, stepping over to the cedar chest. She raised the lid, moved the gray quilt to one side, and lifted out the first of Hope's masterpieces. Henry, Violet, and Jessie helped Lina spread it out while Benny gathered up the delicate old tissue paper in which it had been folded.

Mr. Munsey blinked. He cleared his throat. He leaned close to the quilt, so close his nose almost touched it. Then he whipped a small magnifying glass and a small flashlight from his pocket. He clicked on the light and began to examine the quilt through the magnifying glass.

"Ah, um, hmmm," he murmured as he traced the quilt's stitches with the flashlight and magnifying glass. "Oh, hmmm, yes."

"Yes," he repeated, straightening up. His green eyes were very bright. "Yes, indeed. Treasure, Ms. Diaz. Treasure, indeed. And there are more of these, you say?"

"Five more," Lina said, and she and the Aldens produced the quilts from the cedar chest, one by one.

Mr. Munsey looked at each very, very carefully. "Flying Geese," he murmured. "Log Cabin. Ah . . . the Nine Patch pattern. And look at this stitching, this detail!"

"What are you talking about?" asked Benny.

Mr. Munsey looked up almost as if he'd forgotten anyone else was in the attic with him. "The quilt patterns," he explained. "Those are the names of the patterns of the quilts. This one is called Log Cabin, and that one is Flying Geese."

"I don't see any log cabins or geese flying," said Benny.

"I think I do," said Violet. "I mean, not real geese, but you can see a sort of pattern . . . like the wings of geese when they fly."

"Exactly," said Mr. Munsey. "Both Log Cabin and Flying Geese are very common quilt patterns. A couple of these others are a bit more unusual. All are, well, amazing."

The quilt expert turned to Lina. "Your Great-great-aunt Hope had a wonderful way with color. And I don't think I've ever seen finer stitching. These quilts are worth quite a bit of money."

Lina reached out to stroke a green velvet patch on the Log Cabin quilt. "Yes," she said simply.

"Perhaps you would consider giving them to the museum," said Mr. Munsey. "We could see they are properly cared for and hang them up where many, many people could enjoy them."

With one last quick pat of the quilt, Lina looked up. "Hang them in a museum?" she said. "I don't know."

"They are very valuable. Unique. Irreplaceable. You don't want anything to happen to them, which it easily could, stored in a chest in an attic," said Mr. Munsey. He glanced toward the window. "Even sunlight will damage them."

"The quilts have been here for a long, long time, and they've been safe," Henry pointed out.

Mr. Munsey ignored Henry and kept his attention focused on Lina. "We should act quickly," he urged. "If it's money you want, I can try to arrange something. We're not a wealthy museum, but we have resources."

Laying a hand on Lina's arm, Jessie said, "We'll help you put the quilts back in the trunk, and you can think about it."

"Yes," said Lina. "That's what I'll do. I'll think about it."

"Ms. Diaz, don't take any unnecessary risks," Mr. Munsey said sternly. "Leaving such valuable quilts lying around in an attic is foolish, at best."

"I don't think so, Mr. Munsey," Lina said, smiling sweetly. "And don't worry, I won't take long to make my decision."

"But the quilts," sputtered Mr. Munsey. "The attic could flood. Or catch fire . . . or someone could steal them. As a collector myself, I can tell you that there are many people who would do anything to get a quilt like one of these — even steal one."

"Who's going to steal Hope's quilts? No one knows they're here except us," said Violet.

Mr. Munsey shook his head. "People have ways of finding things out," he said.

"Not if you don't tell anyone," Jessie replied.

Lina began folding the quilts before putting them back into the chest.

"You forgot to look at this quilt," Benny said suddenly. "What about this one?"

Mr. Munsey glanced at the faded gray woolen quilt with rough knots holding it together. "Oh," he said. "That's what is called a hops or utility quilt. Quickly made just to keep someone warm. Very used, not in good condition compared to these other quilts. Look at the different colors of thread where it's been repaired. Odd to find it signed and dated, but it does lend it a certain small value. Nothing compared to these others."

"Maybe she used it every day and liked it because it was so warm and she didn't have to worry about tearing it or spilling anything on it," said Henry.

"Maybe it was her favorite," said Violet. She ran her hand over the worn wool. The fabric wasn't as rough as it looked — in fact, it was soft and warm. The hops quilt was very thick, too, Violet noticed, thicker than the others.

"Most likely it was just put in the trunk

to protect the other quilts," said Mr. Munsey.

After placing the hops quilt inside, Lina shut the trunk and glanced around the attic. It was much emptier than before, and not nearly as dusty. Henry had even cleaned the attic window so the light was brighter.

"Thank you again," Lina said to Mr. Munsey, leading him down the attic stairs to the front door.

"I hope you'll be in touch very soon," said Mr. Munsey. "The sooner you decide to give the quilts to the museum, the sooner they will be safe. Here's my card." He nodded at all the Aldens. "Good day."

"I don't think he's very happy about having to leave those quilts behind," said Henry, once Mr. Munsey was gone.

Lina laughed. "No. But I'll need a lot more information before I make any decisions."

"We'll stop by the library tomorrow to do some research," Jessie promised.

Lina nodded. "Okay. Meanwhile, we've got some signs to make for that yard sale."

*   *   *

The Aldens and Lina sat around the big old table in the dining room of the house and made signs for the yard sale. TREASURES FOR SALE, Jessie wrote in big blue letters on a piece of cardboard. At the bottom of the sign, she wrote Lina's address.

STOP! LOOK! ATTIC SALE AHEAD! Henry printed on a sign to put at the corner of the street.

"After the yard sale, we'll keep looking, won't we?" Benny asked.

"For what?" Violet asked. She was painting all her signs in purple, her favorite color.

"The hidden treasure," said Benny. "Hope's treasure."

"Wouldn't that be amazing," Lina said. "To find that treasure, whatever it is — if there is one."

"There is," said Benny. "I know there is."

"Well, first we'll put these signs up all over town tomorrow," said Jessie.

"I have some business in Silver City tomorrow," Lina said. "I'll put some up there,

too. And I'll put an advertisement in the newspapers."

"It's going to be a great yard sale!" said Benny. "I can hardly wait."

Waving good-bye, the Aldens headed home.

"Do you think it's true what the quilt man said?" asked Benny as they walked. "That someone might want to steal Lina's quilts?"

"No," said Jessie. "No one's going to bother Lina or the quilts."

Henry agreed. "I think Mr. Munsey was just trying to scare Lina into giving up the quilts right away."

Jessie made a face. "I didn't like the way he tried to pressure her into it. I wonder why he's so anxious to get the quilts immediately."

"Maybe she *should* give the quilts to the museum, just to keep them safe," said Violet.

"They're safe," said Jessie. "Don't worry. No one's going to try to steal them. No one even knows they're here!"

CHAPTER 4

Burglars and Bargains

The Aldens were on their way
to the library the next morning when a
green van pulled up next to them. It was
Lina, and she didn't have her usual smile on
her face.

"Good morning!" Henry called. Then he
noticed the worried look on Lina's face.
"What's wrong?" he asked.

"Someone tried to break into my house
last night," said Lina.

Violet gasped. "Oh, no!"

"Oh, yes," said Lina.

"Who was it?" asked Benny.

"Did they steal the quilts?" asked Violet at the same time.

"I don't know who it was, and no, nothing got stolen," Lina answered. "The thief never made it inside. Whoever it was tried to force open the back door. But the lock is strong and the noise woke me up. I turned on the lights and went down to investigate, but whoever it was had run off."

"The lights must have scared him — or her — away," said Jessie.

"I think you're right," said Lina.

"Do you think the burglar knew about the hidden treasure?" asked Benny.

"Or the quilts?" said Violet.

"Maybe. Maybe not," said Lina. "But it is strange that suddenly, on the very day that Mr. Munsey told me how valuable those quilts are, someone tried to break into the house."

"Yes," agreed Henry. "Very strange."

Benny frowned. "Do you think it could have been Mr. Munsey?"

Lina shook her head. "I just don't know,"

she said. "I reported it to the police, and they're going to keep an eye on things. I asked the neighbors to keep their eyes peeled, too. Meanwhile, I'm going to get an extra lock for each door, just in case."

"Good idea," said Henry.

After Lina had driven away, Jessie said, "Maybe we should talk to Mr. Munsey."

"Yes! We'll ask him if he tried to steal the quilts," said Benny.

"Well, I don't think we'll ask him that," Henry said. "It's possible whoever tried to break in doesn't even know about the quilts. But we *will* try to find out if he told anyone about them."

Jessie nodded. "If anyone besides us knows about the quilts, Mr. Munsey must have told them."

Violet's eyes widened. "Maybe Mr. Munsey told someone so they could steal the quilts for him."

Benny hopped excitedly from one foot to the other. "We're going to solve a mystery!"

Jessie smiled at her little brother. "First,

let's do our research — that will help Lina, too."

When the Aldens reached Greenfield library, Jessie and Benny went to find books on quilts while Henry and Violet looked up quilts on the computer.

Soon Jessie and Benny had made a small pile of books on a table in a quiet corner of the library.

"We have lots of books," said Benny.

"Yes, but most of them are about how to make quilts," said Jessie. "We need to know about the quilts' history and how much they're worth." She handed Benny some of the books. "Why don't you look through these?"

"Okay," said Benny. He opened the first book and looked at the pictures. Benny could read a little, but not much yet.

A few minutes later, Benny said, "I found something! Here's a picture of a quilt like one of the ones in the attic." He pointed at the page.

" 'Flying Geese, a traditional pattern,' "

Jessie read over Benny's shoulder. "It says the quilt in the picture is over a hundred years old and it's hanging in a museum in New York. It says the quilt is valuable because of its age and condition, the skill of its maker, and the fact that it's signed and dated."

Benny nodded as if he already knew all that. "That's what makes Hope's quilts worth a lot, too," he said.

They found several more photographs of quilts much like the ones in the attic. Then they joined Violet and Henry, who were printing pages and pages of quilt facts they'd found on the computer.

"Mr. Munsey was telling the truth," Violet announced, "at least about how valuable the quilts are. People buy and sell old quilts for lots of money — and most aren't nearly as pretty as the ones we found."

"Who buys them?" Benny asked.

"Museums and private collectors," said Henry. "We read about auctions where people paid thousands of dollars for quilts."

"That's lots of money," said Benny, his eyes growing round.

"Yes," agreed Jessie. "If Lina wanted to sell the quilts, she could be rich."

"And look what else we found," said Violet. "This is called a Wedding Ring quilt. See? The pattern is of all these connected circles that look like rings."

"I wonder if that's the kind of quilt Lina's Great-great-aunt Hope made for her own wedding," said Jessie.

"And I wonder what happened to it," Henry said.

"Maybe she gave it away because it was too sad for her when she looked at it," Violet said.

"Maybe," said Jessie. "Or maybe her wedding quilt is the treasure that people say she hid."

Henry jumped up and began to gather books and papers. "Let's check out a few of these books," he said. "Then let's go home and — "

"Have a snack?" asked Benny.

Henry smiled. "A snack," he agreed. "And we'll call Mr. Munsey, too."

As they headed home, Benny said, "Someone should make a snack quilt."

"Or cake," said Violet.

"But real snacks are better," said Benny. Working at the library had made him hungry.

While the others prepared the snack, Henry called Mr. Munsey.

He hung up the phone, looking discouraged. "He's not there," he reported. "I told his assistant that we met him at Lina's house and said I had some questions about quilts. The assistant said she'd tell Mr. Munsey we called, but I don't think she knew who Lina was — I had to repeat her name three times."

"It doesn't sound as if Mr. Munsey told anyone about the quilts we found," said Violet.

"At least not his assistant," said Jessie.

The children ate their snack and headed to Lina's house to show her what they had discovered at the library. They had just rounded the corner onto Lina's block when Henry stopped short.

"What's wrong?" Violet asked.

Henry stepped behind a bush and motioned for his brother and sisters to follow. "Look," he said in a hushed voice.

The others turned and saw a small, beat-up old car parked directly across the street from Lina's house.

"Who's that inside?" asked Benny.

"I don't know," said Henry. "But whoever it is, he's wearing dark glasses — and he seems to be watching the house."

CHAPTER 5

Long Lost Letters

"Let's watch for a minute," Violet said in a low voice. "Maybe he'll drive away soon."

"Or maybe he's after the hidden treasure," said Benny.

The Aldens peered at the car. Inside, the man with dark glasses sat, his head turned toward Lina's house, his chin bobbing up and down as if in time to music.

"He must have the radio on," Jessie whispered.

Suddenly, the man raised a camera and

peered through the lens, turning his head and the camera as if the camera was a pair of binoculars.

The Aldens ducked.

When they peeked out again, the man had put the camera down.

"A spy," breathed Benny.

Just then another car pulled up. It was newer and nicer. A woman in a suit with a puffy scarf tied around her neck got out and marched toward the first car. She tapped on the window, and the man in the car jumped in surprise. A moment later, he got out, and the two began to talk.

Mostly, she talked and he nodded. He kept nodding as he bent into the backseat, pulled out an enormous video camera, and began to fiddle with it.

The woman tossed back her thick black hair and marched toward Lina's house.

"Come on!" said Jessie.

The Aldens jumped out of their hiding place and raced toward the woman.

"Regina, wait," they heard the man say.

But the woman kept walking. As she

reached the gate, the Aldens stepped in front of her. "Excuse me," Jessie said politely.

The woman stopped. The man with the camera stopped.

"Do you live here?" the woman asked.

"Here? No," Henry said.

"Do you know anything about the hidden treasure?" the woman interrupted.

Violet's mouth dropped open.

"Hidden treasure!" exclaimed Benny. "How did you . . ."

"Shh, Benny," Violet whispered, and Benny clapped one hand over his mouth.

"A hidden treasure, that's what I heard. And I want the story!" The woman pushed past the Aldens and continued her march to the house. Before they could stop her, she was knocking on the front door.

Lina opened it.

"Regina Lott," the woman said briskly, offering Lina her hand. "DocuNews Reports."

"What?" said Lina.

"I've come to set up an exclusive interview for my feature story about this hidden treasure of yours," Regina went on. She said over her shoulder, "Tom, camera!"

The man in the dark glasses raised his video camera.

Lina held up a hand. "Just a minute," she said. "What is all this about?"

"Hidden treasure. Valuable antiques. Rare quilts. It's quite a story," said Regina.

"How did you find out?" Violet gasped.

"I have my sources," Regina said with a smirk.

"What did Mr. Munsey tell you?" demanded Jessie.

Regina looked at Jessie blankly for a moment. "Who?" she asked. Then she turned to Lina. "Never mind. Back to the story. You're cleaning this house you just bought, this old, abandoned house, searching for a hidden treasure, and . . . "

"No one in my family ever really believed that old story," said Lina.

" . . . and there in a hidden drawer . . . " Regina continued, then paused, as if she expected someone else to finish the sentence.

"What hidden drawer?" asked Benny. "The quilts weren't in a hidden drawer." Then he clapped his hand over his mouth.

"Quilts," said Regina. "Ah, yes, quilts. Are they as rare and valuable as you hoped?" As she asked the question, Regina raised a small microphone toward Lina.

"Wait a minute," said Henry, who had just noticed that the cameraman was filming them.

"Valuable quilts. A hidden treasure," Regina went on. "Are you going to sell the quilts to fix up this house and make it into your dream home?"

"No!" said Lina. "At least, not all of them."

"So they *are* valuable!" said Regina triumphantly. "What about the other treasure? Is it jewelry? Gold?"

Looking alarmed, Lina said, "We haven't found anything like that."

Regina lowered the microphone. "Listen," she said. "I'm going to do this story with your help or without it. If you help me, you can tell it the way you want it."

Violet spoke up. "What about the yard sale? Will you put that in your story?"

Regina tossed her thick hair. It was a gesture she seemed to enjoy. "What yard sale?"

"There's a yard sale right here on Saturday, with lots of things we found in the house and attic," Violet explained.

"Including the quilts?" asked Regina.

"Those aren't for sale. But we found lots of other amazing stuff," Jessie said.

"Show me some of this, er, amazing stuff, and I might give you some very good publicity for your yard sale," said Regina. She added, "If you show me the quilts, too."

Henry glanced at Lina.

Lina sighed. "Oh, all right. Follow me."

She led the way to the attic.

Regina didn't sneeze. She stalked around the attic, peering at everything.

"I'll show you the quilts," said Lina, "but please, don't put them in the story about the yard sale, because they aren't for sale."

Regina tapped her chin with one long, painted fingernail. "Hmmm. Well, if you'll let me take some good footage of the quilts now, I'll do a quick report on your yard sale. We'll just say treasures from your attic are going to be in the yard sale and leave it at that, okay?"

She talked so fast that it made Violet's head spin.

Lina blinked, then said slowly, "Okay, that seems fair."

Once again, Lina and the Aldens unpacked the quilts.

Tom raised the camera, Regina asked questions, and Lina answered as best she could.

Finally, Regina motioned to Tom to turn off the camera. "Not bad," she said. "These quilts will make a good story later — once you've decided what to do with them."

Just then Benny, who'd been leaning against the trunk, said, "Oh!"

At the same moment, the trunk began to tip over backward.

"Benny!" shrieked Violet.

Benny saved himself from falling by grabbing Jessie's arm. Henry grabbed the top of the trunk right before it toppled.

There was a ripping sound.

Everyone froze.

"The quilts," whispered Violet.

But it wasn't a quilt that had ripped. It was the thin silk lining in the lid of the trunk.

"I'm sorry," Henry began, then stopped. He reached down and pulled a folded sheet of paper from the tear in the silk.

He handed it to Lina. She unfolded it carefully. After a long moment she said, "It's a letter."

Jessie peered over Lina's shoulder at the beautiful old-fashioned handwriting. She saw the signature at the bottom. "Robert," she said.

"It's one of the letters Robert wrote to Hope," said Lina.

"Letters?" Regina tried to push forward to see the letter.

"There are more," said Henry. One by one he carefully pulled more than a dozen letters from the torn silk lining.

"What is this?" Regina demanded.

In a dazed voice, Lina told Regina the

story of Robert and Hope and the wedding that never happened.

"Now, this is shaping into a story," Regina said. "What do the letters say?"

"I'll have to read them first," Lina said. "Later."

"When you do," Regina said, "it's my story, okay?"

Lina nodded, but she hardly seemed to be paying attention. She held on to the letters all the way down the stairs and to the front door.

They all watched as Regina stopped at the bottom of the stairs, raised her microphone, and said, "So, viewers, if you want treasure, this is the place. I've seen an attic full of it, and it's going to be on sale here this Saturday in Greenfield. I'm Regina Lott, DocuNews Reports."

She switched off the microphone, and Tom lowered the camera. "Okay, I'll be back," she called over her shoulder as she walked outside. "Come on, Tom," she said. A moment later, they were gone.

Lina walked back to the kitchen and sat

down with the letters. She spread them out.

She looked around at the Aldens. "You helped find these letters," she said. "So you should help read them."

The Aldens gathered around Lina, eager to hear what the letters said. Lina read them aloud, one by one, thirteen in all.

In them, Robert described the places he saw and the people he met as he traveled. He told Hope over and over how much he missed her and looked forward to coming home.

"Listen!" Lina exclaimed. She read aloud, " 'And how is our Wedding Ring quilt? Is it finished yet?' "

"So there *was* a wedding quilt," said Henry.

"We saw Wedding Ring quilts at the library," Benny told Lina. "Pictures of them."

As she read the next letter, Lina said, "Here's more about the quilt, I think. It says, 'I remember how the wedding ring matches your eyes, that rare and beautiful color. It is a shade of green that will always be my favorite.' "

"So green wasn't just Hope's favorite color," said Lina, "it was also the color of her eyes."

"And she made her wedding quilt to match," Violet added.

The letters were not very long, and soon they'd come to the end of them. In the thirteenth letter, Robert mentioned that he wasn't feeling well. It was his last letter to Hope.

The Aldens and Lina sat silently for awhile. Then Lina folded the letters. "I'm going to put these in my desk and lock it," she said. "Thank you for finding them. It's even better than finding those quilts."

As they headed home, Benny said, "We solved a little mystery, didn't we? We found the letters."

"Yes, I guess we did," said Henry.

"But we still don't know who tried to break into Lina's house," Jessie reminded them.

Violet nodded. "Yes. And who told Regina Lott about the quilts and the hidden treasure?"

"It had to be Mr. Munsey," said Benny.

"She didn't seem to know who Mr. Munsey was," Jessie said.

"Maybe she was just pretending she didn't know him," said Benny.

"Could be," said Henry. "But why would Mr. Munsey tell her?"

"I don't know," said Jessie, frowning. "It doesn't make sense. He was worried about the quilts being safe. If everyone knows they are in the attic, they won't be as safe."

"Maybe that's why," said Violet. "Mr. Munsey wants to convince Lina to give the quilts to the museum, so . . ."

"So maybe he told Regina about them and tried to make it look as if someone was breaking into Lina's house, so she'd worry the quilts were in danger," finished Jessie.

"Yeah!" said Benny.

"Hmm," said Henry.

"Someone else at the museum could have told Regina about the quilts, too," Jessie pointed out.

"True," said Henry. He sighed. "We can do a little more investigating after the yard sale tomorrow. We'll have more time, then."

"And maybe more clues," Benny added.

The next morning, the Aldens ate a quick breakfast, then went to Lina's house to help set up the yard sale. But when Jessie knocked on the front door, nobody answered.

"Knock some more," said Henry. "Lina's got to be here. The yard sale starts soon."

Jessie knocked again. Finally, Lina opened the door. "Quick! Inside," she said.

They hurried inside the house. "What's wrong?" Violet asked.

"Is someone trying to break in again?" asked Benny.

"No! Unless you count the people who were already here for the yard sale. They started knocking on my door practically at dawn this morning. Dawn!" said Lina.

"But the sign says the yard sale starts at nine," said Violet.

Lina made a face. "People are excited because of Regina's little story on the news last night. Didn't you see it?"

The Aldens exchanged glances. "No," said Henry.

"Well, you didn't miss much," said Lina. "The whole thing only lasted about fifteen seconds, but I guess that was enough to — "

Knocking on the front door interrupted her.

"The yard sale doesn't start until nine," Lina said in a loud voice without opening the door. "You'll have to wait until then."

"We'll start putting the tables and stuff out now," Henry said. "If we work together, we'll have it done in no time."

But they didn't have a chance to work together. No sooner had Henry set up the first table and Jessie brought out the first box than all four doors of a car parked out front flew open. People spilled out and hurried toward them. "This the yard sale? Where's the treasure?" the man in the lead asked, looking around.

"Treasure?" Henry repeated, startled.

"We saw the story on the news last night. 'Treasure house holds yard sale,' the reporter said," the man told Henry. " '*Hidden* treasures,' she said."

"We're not ready yet," Jessie said politely. "The sale starts at nine."

"Early bird gets the worm, right?" said the man. He reached for the box Jessie had just put down. "You don't mind if I just go through this box a little early, do you?"

"Yes!" said Jessie. "Please stop."

The man stopped, frowning.

Henry said, "You'd better stay with the stuff, Jessie. I'll tell Lina, and she can come help you."

"Good idea," said Jessie. Keeping a sharp eye on the man, she began to unpack the box.

As Henry went back up the walk, he heard Jessie say firmly, "I'm sorry, but we're not selling anything until nine A.M. If you want to wait, you will have to wait outside the front gate."

Henry smiled. Jessie was in charge, and he was sure the yard sale was going to be a big success.

CHAPTER 6

Sales and Snoops

"I just sold a box of old towels," Violet reported, handing Lina the money. Lina was sitting at one of the tables with a metal box for the money. She was the yard sale treasurer. The Aldens were walking among all the boxes, tables, chairs, lamps, and other items for sale, helping the shoppers.

"This is great!" Jessie said, coming to join them. "We've barely been here an hour, and just look at all these people!"

"All the signs you put up helped," Lina

said. "In fact, I couldn't have done this without you."

Violet blushed. "Thanks," she said. "But it wasn't just us. Regina Lott gets some credit, too. A lot of people saw that story she did."

A customer came up to pay for two flower-pots, and Violet let her gaze wander around the crowded yard sale. She noticed a short, bouncy-looking man who seemed to be looking as much at Lina as at the things for sale. He picked up an old vase, looked at the bottom of it, then put it down. He looked around again, then walked toward the house and moved partway behind an overgrown bush.

Violet frowned and stood up.

The man slipped out from behind the bush, glanced over his shoulder, then disappeared from sight around the corner of the house.

What was he doing? Where was he going? Violet turned to tell Lina, but Lina was busy helping another customer. Quickly,

Violet walked toward where the man had disappeared.

Henry caught up with her. "What's wrong?" he said.

"Someone just went around the side of the house," Violet said.

"We should check it out," Henry said.

With Henry leading the way, the two of them hurried after the man.

"Maybe he's just using the shortcut back to his house," Henry said.

"I don't think so," Violet said. "He acted as if he didn't want anyone to see him."

They saw no sign of the man in the backyard.

"Hmm," said Henry. He turned and Violet followed as he walked up the back steps. The door to the kitchen was unlocked. Henry pushed it open.

The two Aldens slipped quietly inside and listened.

Muffled footsteps sounded on the stairs.

"Come on," said Henry in a low voice.

Still moving as silently as they could,

Henry and Violet rushed to the bottom of the staircase just as the man bounced out of sight. They heard a door open and close, more footsteps, then another door open.

Henry and Violet tiptoed up the stairs. The door at the end of the hall stood ajar.

Violet ran to the door and pushed through it just as the bouncy man was opening a closet door to peer inside.

"What are you doing?" asked Henry.

"Oh!" cried the man. He jumped, letting the door slam, then turned to face them.

He was dressed in an old navy jacket, neat khakis, and a pale blue shirt with a little animal stitched on the pocket. He was wearing very white, very clean sneakers.

The man gave Violet and Henry a hurt look. "You scared me," he said.

"We're sorry we scared you, but what are you doing in Lina's house?" asked Violet.

The man sighed. "It's a nice house," he said.

"But you have no right to be in here," said Henry.

"I'm . . . looking for the bathroom," the man said.

"It's downstairs, right past where you came in," Violet said. "The door was open. You couldn't miss it."

The man's eyebrows went up. He reached out, picked up a small mirror on a nearby table, and turned it over to look at it. "Was it?" he said, putting the mirror down. "I must have missed it."

"We'll show you where it is," Henry said, stepping back and holding the door open.

"No, no, that won't be necessary," said the man, going past with his odd, bouncy step. He bounded down the steps and around the corner down the hall. Henry and Violet had to move fast to keep up. They barely made it to the kitchen before the back door slammed shut behind the odd visitor.

"How strange," said Violet.

"Yes," agreed Henry. "And I don't think he really was looking for the bathroom."

Violet and Henry locked the door carefully behind them and headed back to the yard sale.

People were everywhere. But the bouncy man was nowhere to be seen.

"Where have you been?" Jessie cried as they walked toward her. She was kneeling, pulling boxes from beneath a table. "We need to put the rest of these books out on this table. And Lina needs someone to be the treasurer while she takes a break. And — "

An elderly couple interrupted her to ask the price of a lamp.

"I'll help with the books," Henry said.

Violet nodded. "I'll give Lina a break," she said. She added in a lower voice, "We can tell them about the bouncy man when the yard sale is over."

By noon, most of the things were sold, and Lina's cash box was full of money. People still kept coming, though, and asking about the treasure.

At last, Henry made a sign that said YARD SALE OVER, put it on the fence, and shut the gate tight.

"I think we can begin counting the money," Lina said.

"Let's put everything we didn't sell into a box and just give it away," said Benny.

"Good idea," said Lina. "We can leave the box outside the gate."

Henry picked up a big cardboard box and walked to the nearest table.

"I'll help," said Benny. He hurried over to the table and scooped a deck of cards and some magazines into the box. At the next table, they piled in some small, chipped dishes.

At the third table, they found a woman with curly red hair kneeling by a box of old clothes.

"Oh!" said Benny when he saw the woman.

The woman looked up and smiled. "How much for this box of old clothes?" she said.

"We were going to put it all in our free box," Benny said. "The yard sale is over."

"I wish I could have gotten here sooner, but I couldn't leave work," the woman said. She looked down at the box. "Free is good, but let me at least pay something. Do you think two dollars is fair?"

"Sure," said Henry. "You can pay Lina. She's over there."

"I'll do that," the woman said, with a smile. She had brown eyes that crinkled at the corners. "If you don't mind, I'd like to look through a couple more boxes."

"Okay," said Benny.

Henry and Benny finished filling their box and left it outside the gate under a sign that said FREE. Then they walked back to the table where Lina, Jessie, and Violet stood. The red-haired woman was still there, too. She had the box of old clothes propped on one hip. An old basket stood at her feet.

Benny looked down at the basket. It was full of cut-up bits of clothes and torn rags.

"Are you buying that, too?" he asked.

The woman nodded and smiled. "I can use the scraps," she said. She paused, then said, "So, is this all that you're selling?"

"Well, for the time being," said Lina. "I still have rooms of furniture I need to go through, and a few other things to sort out."

The woman studied Lina, then glanced down at the basket, as if she might be about to say something in reply. But she didn't.

"I could help you carry the box and the basket to your car," Henry offered.

"No, no, no, thank you. I'm strong from all the lifting I do at my store," the woman said.

"Store?" said Benny.

"I'm Coral Weaver, owner of Weaver Stitch Shop," said the woman. "I sell everything for people who like to sew. And I'm one of the founding members of the Crazy Quilters Club." She patted the box. "That's what these scraps are for. They'll make a great quilt."

"Crazy quilters?" said Benny.

"We read about crazy quilts at the library, Benny, remember?" said Violet. "They're quilts without a pattern, made of all kinds and shapes of cloth stitched together."

"That's right!" Coral said, looking pleased. "You like quilts?"

"Yes," said Violet. "They're beautiful."

"Lina's Great-great-aunt Hope was a crazy quilter, too," said Benny. "But her quilts are all made from patterns."

"I'd love to see them," Coral said. She gave Lina a hopeful look.

"Maybe some other time," said Lina.

"If they're still up in the attic, I don't mind climbing stairs," Coral said. "Really, I don't."

Lina looked startled. "How did you know they're in the attic?" she said.

"I love quilts," Coral said, ignoring the question. "The old ones are so beautiful, so full of stories — I always wonder about the lives of the women who made them. There's a story in every stitch. Stories of engagements, weddings, births, friendships, even deaths." Coral smiled. "It's kind of crazy, I know, but then, some people do call me the crazy quilt lady. Get it? Crazy quilt lady?"

Lina smiled back. "I love quilts, too," she said.

Coral sighed. "Well, I'd better be going. But come to my shop. I'll tell you everything you need to know about quilts. I'll even show you how to make one."

"That would be fun," said Jessie.

"Is it hard?" asked Violet.

"Not at all," said Coral. "Nothing you love to do is hard, don't you know?"

"I never thought about it that way," said Jessie.

"South Street, just around the corner from the bank," Coral said as she picked up her basket. "Come anytime."

"We will," Jessie promised.

Coral nodded, smiled one last time, and headed for her car.

As the gate swung closed behind Coral, Lina snapped the cash box shut.

"Crazy quilt lady," she said. She shook her head. "That's the way I'm beginning to feel, too."

CHAPTER 7

Without a Clue

"Lina," Violet said as the Aldens followed Lina to the house, "there's something Henry and I need to tell you."

Henry nodded solemnly. He and Violet quickly filled in the others on the man with the bouncy walk who had sneaked into Lina's house during the yard sale.

When they had finished the story, Jessie asked, "Do you think it was the same person who tried to break in before?"

"Could be," said Henry. "He was definitely searching for something, and I'm pretty sure it wasn't the bathroom."

"He was looking in the closet and at the stuff on your dresser," Violet added.

"Bouncy walk, bushy eyebrows, neat dresser, did you say? He didn't buy anything," Lina said, "or I'd have remembered him."

"I noticed him at the yard sale. He inspected all of the china and vases really carefully," Jessie said.

Just then the phone rang. Lina dashed into the house to answer it. Through the open door, the Aldens heard her say, "Yes, Regina, of course I remember you. No, not today, I'm too tired. Tomorrow isn't good for me, either. No. No! Fine, call me Monday morning. Good-bye."

Lina came out, shaking her head. "That reporter, she doesn't give up. She keeps pestering me to let her into the attic again and tell her more about the quilts."

Benny, who had been thinking hard, said suddenly, "I saw him. That bouncy man. I saw him with Coral."

"You did?" said Henry. Everyone looked at Benny.

"Yes. During the yard sale," said Benny.

"When? Coral didn't get to the yard sale until late," Henry said. "The man was gone by then."

Benny thought, then said, "It wasn't late, but it wasn't early. I saw him arrive. He got out of her car, and she drove away."

"Benny, are you sure?" Violet said.

Benny nodded firmly. "I remember her red hair."

"Well, Coral did know that the quilts were in the attic," Jessie said. "If she and that man are in this together, that explains it . . . unless it was a lucky guess."

Lina sighed. "A crazy quilt lady, a bouncy snoop, a mysterious wannabe burglar, *and* a news reporter who won't take no for an answer," she said. "Maybe I should just call Mr. Munsey and tell him to take the quilts, at least for now."

"But what if Mr. Munsey is the one who told the burglar about the quilts? Or what if he *is* the burglar?" Violet said. "Remember, he's the only one we told — and then Regina showed up."

"Let's try to talk to Mr. Munsey," said Henry. "We'll visit Coral at her shop, too, and see if we can pick up any clues."

"Meanwhile, I think we should hide the quilts," Jessie said, "to keep them safe."

"Where?" asked Violet.

"I think I have an idea," Jessie said. "Come on!"

A short time later, she was smoothing one side of the old hops quilt while Violet tugged and straightened the corner of the other side.

All six quilts had been layered on the bed in the room across the hall from Lina's. The old hops quilt was spread out over them.

"No one will think to look for more quilts underneath this old one," said Lina. "Good idea, Jessie."

"And no one will be able to sneak by, even if they do get in to steal the quilts," said Benny. "This floor is nice and creaky!"

"Yes," agreed Jessie. "One way or another, the quilts will be safe."

* * *

As the Aldens walked home from Lina's, they discussed what to do next. "The museum closes early on Saturdays," Jessie said. "That means Mr. Munsey won't be there now."

"Then we can't ask him any questions, at least today," Henry said.

Violet sighed. "And we don't know who Mr. Bouncy is," she said, "or where to find him."

"The crazy quilt lady does," Benny said.

"You're right, Benny," said Jessie. "She does. Let's hurry down to her shop before it closes for the day."

"Come on!" said Henry.

The Aldens ran the rest of the way home and hopped on their bicycles. Pedaling fast, they were soon downtown.

"There's Weaver Stitch Shop," Violet said. She led the way to a bike rack on the corner.

"Look!" said Violet. "Mr. Bouncy."

The Aldens stared as a neatly dressed man in a polo shirt and khakis walked out

the door of the Stitch Shop. He bobbed across the street, pushed open the door of another shop, and went inside. Jessie looked at the fancy gold lettering on the shop's window and read aloud, "Grey's Fine Antiques."

"You were right, Benny. Coral does know that man," Henry said.

"But who is he?" asked Benny.

"Let's go find out," Jessie said.

They went into the Stitch Shop to find Coral sitting in a worn overstuffed chair with the basket of scraps at her feet. There were no customers.

Coral looked up and gave a little start as they came in.

"Oh!" she said. She laughed but it sounded forced. "You came to visit a lot more quickly than I expected."

"Have you found any good scraps?" asked Violet.

"Good scraps? Oh, these." Coral looked down at the basket, then looked away. She seemed jumpy.

"Is everything okay?" asked Jessie.

"Of course, of course," said Coral. She nudged the basket to one side with her foot and stood up. "How do you like my shop?" she asked.

They looked around. It was a colorful place with cozy chairs, a bright quilt on one wall, racks of thread and sewing supplies, a cabinet labeled PATTERNS, another labeled PROJECTS, and lots and lots of cloth.

"What's that up there?" asked Benny, pointing to a large wooden frame that looked sort of like a bed frame. It was suspended from the ceiling above them.

"That? That's a quilting frame," Coral said. "You stretch the top and bottom of a quilt across it and stitch them together. At least that's one way to do it. I can raise and lower it when I need to, so it doesn't take up room in the shop."

"This place is wonderful," Violet said. She ran her fingers across some pretty purple cloth and thought she might like to make a quilt in that color, to match the violet flowers on her wallpaper.

Coral talked some more about quilting,

and all four of the Aldens asked lots of questions. The more she talked, the more excited Coral got. She knew the answer to every question.

"I think she must know as much as Mr. Munsey," Jessie said softly to Henry.

"Maybe more," Henry whispered back. To Coral, he said, "Do many men make quilts?"

"More and more," Coral said. She didn't seem so nervous now.

"I wondered," Henry went on, "because we saw a man coming out of your shop, and we were wondering if he makes quilts."

Coral thought for a moment. "A man coming of the shop this afternoon?" she said slowly.

"Yes, just before we came in. He has short hair and thick eyebrows, and he walks with a sort of bounce," said Violet.

"Oh! That's Dirk Grey," said Coral. "He owns the antique shop across the street."

"We thought we saw him at the yard sale this morning, too," Violet said.

"Yes, he was at the sale," Coral said. "I

gave him a ride — well, a ride from his car. He'd parked down the street from the house because there were so many other cars, and I decided to take a look at where the sale was on my way to my store." Coral smiled.

"Oh," said Benny, and the disappointment in his voice mirrored what the others were feeling. There was nothing suspicious about Coral Weaver and Dirk Grey meeting before the sale that morning.

"I know a man who likes quilts," Jessie said. "Mr. Munsey. Do you know him?"

"The name doesn't sound familiar," Coral said, "but I'm terrible with names."

"Oh," Jessie said, her voice as disappointed as Benny's.

"Well, thank you for dropping by," Coral said, suddenly sounding as if she was in a hurry. "Come again." She followed the Aldens to the door — and closed it behind them. When Jessie glanced back, she saw Coral hang up the CLOSED sign.

"I got the feeling that Coral wanted us out of there all of the sudden," said Henry.

"Yes, me, too!" Jessie exclaimed. "And look — according to the sign, the store should be open for another half hour."

"She *was* acting funny," Benny said, "especially when we came in."

"But she seemed to like talking about quiltmaking," Violet pointed out.

"You're right," said Jessie. She paused, then added, "Maybe she was nervous when we got there because of Mr. Grey. He'd just left, remember?"

"Could be," Henry said. "And maybe she wanted us to leave before we could ask her more about him."

"I think we should talk to Mr. Grey," said Jessie.

"Hold my hand while we cross the street, Benny," Violet said. She led the way.

Dirk Grey's shop was still open, and they could see him inside, sitting behind a desk. Jessie pushed open the door and went inside.

Mr. Grey looked up. The smile on his lips faded when he saw Violet and Henry with Jessie and Benny.

"May I help you?" he said, his voice cool.

"Hello, Mr. Grey," said Henry.

Mr. Grey glanced at the lettering on his window and nodded. "You're right. I'm Dirk Grey, and this is my shop." He stopped and waited.

"You were at our yard sale this morning. In the house," Henry said.

"I was," agreed Mr. Grey.

"What were you looking for?" asked Jessie.

The man shrugged. "I'm an antique dealer. I was curious to see if there was anything in the house that I might want to buy." He paused. "Old clothes, furniture, knickknacks, quilts, maybe. Anything of value."

"You shouldn't have gone sneaking in like that," said Violet. "You should have asked."

"Maybe not, but it didn't do any harm," said Mr. Grey. He didn't sound at all sorry.

"You don't know anyone named Edward Munsey, do you?" Jessie asked suddenly.

"Munsey?" Mr. Grey repeated. His eyes shifted. Then he said, "Antique dealer?"

"No," said Jessie. "He works for the state museum."

"Ah. I thought the name sounded slightly familiar," said Mr. Grey. "I have friends who own antique shops near that museum. That's probably where I heard it."

The phone on Mr. Grey's desk rang. He reached for it. "If you'll excuse me," he said to the Aldens. "Have a nice day."

There was nothing to do but leave.

Henry, Jessie, Benny, and Violet headed for home. They didn't pedal as fast this time. They didn't have to hurry. They could talk as they rode their bikes.

"I don't like Mr. Grey," said Benny.

"He doesn't seem very honest," Henry agreed.

"He admitted to sneaking into Lina's house to look around," Violet added.

"But was he really looking for the quilts? I didn't notice any quilts in his shop, just furniture and lots of china and glass," Jessie said.

"You're right!" said Violet.

"Maybe he was searching for the hidden treasure," Benny said.

"I think he *does* know who Mr. Munsey is," Henry said. "I don't think he told us the truth."

"Do you think Mr. Grey and Mr. Munsey could be working together? Mr. Grey could have been the one who tried to break in . . . " Jessie's voice trailed off.

"To get the quilts for Mr. Munsey," Henry finished for her. "But how does Regina Lott fit in all this? How did she hear about the quilts and the treasure?"

"And what *is* the treasure?" Benny added.

"What about Coral?" asked Violet. "She's a quilt expert, too, but she doesn't know Mr. Munsey. Or at least she says she doesn't."

"And she was acting strange when we were in her shop," agreed Jessie.

"Coral has a nice smile," said Benny. "I like her."

"But everyone is a suspect, Benny,"

Henry said firmly. "Coral *did* seem to know about the quilts in the attic."

"Maybe Mr. Munsey told Dirk Grey, and he told Coral, and she's the one who's after the quilts!" said Jessie.

"It does seem like a stretch," Jessie said. She sighed.

"We have suspects and clues, but nothing that puts them together," Violet said.

"It's like a quilt without a pattern," said Benny.

"Exactly like that," said Henry. "A crazy quilt mystery."

CHAPTER 8

Hide-and-Seek

"We've only got a few more signs to take down and then we'll be finished," said Henry. He handed Jessie one of the yard sale posters they'd put up only a few days before.

"Good," said Benny. "I'm *tired*."

Just then, a familiar green van pulled up.

"I thought I'd find you somewhere around here," Lina said, leaning out the van window. "I'm glad I caught you."

"Hi," said Benny.

"Is everything okay?" asked Jessie. "Did someone try to break in again?"

"No, nothing like that. Coral Weaver called and said she needed to talk to me about something important, something to do with the yard sale. I thought you might like to come along."

"Yes," said Henry instantly.

"We'll get the rest of the signs later," agreed Jessie, crumpling up the one she was holding and dropping it into the recycling can at the curb.

The Aldens jumped into the van and headed for Coral's store. The door was propped open, and Coral called from inside the store as they walked up, "Come in, come in."

Coral was perched on one of the store's comfy chairs, focusing on a small square of quilted fabric in her lap.

"Are you making a quilt?" Violet asked politely.

"A quilted cover for a pillow," Coral said. "To protect it and keep all of the feathers from leaking out. It's a gift for a friend."

"What a nice gift," said Lina.

Coral looked up. "Yes," she said. She set her quilting work to one side. She took a deep breath.

"I have something I think you should see," Coral said quietly. She got up and went to the back of the shop. When she returned, she was holding the old basket she'd bought at the yard sale.

"The scrap basket," said Jessie.

"That's right," Coral said. "But it had more than scraps in it."

"Treasure!" said Benny hopefully.

"Of a sort," said Coral.

She reached into the basket and brought out a few folded sheets of yellow paper.

"More letters?" Lina said, her voice going up in excitement.

"No," said Coral. "Look."

Carefully, she unfolded the fragile papers and spread them out on a nearby table. The papers were full of lines and drawings, notes and sketches.

"These papers were Hope's," Violet said. "Look, she signed her name in that corner."

Lina looked bewildered. "What does all this mean?" she asked.

"It looks like . . . is it a quilting pattern?" Henry asked.

"Yes, a Wedding Ring quilt pattern," said Coral. She pulled a book from the shelf by her chair and flipped it open. "Like this one."

Lina was looking at Hope's signature. "It's dated," she said. "This pattern has a date on it. It must be the pattern for Hope's wedding quilt."

"The missing quilt," Violet said softly.

"I found it underneath the scraps, right after I got home," said Coral. "I wanted to keep it. I thought how wonderful it would look hanging in my store, framed. But that would have been wrong. It belongs to you."

Lina stared down at the pattern unfolded on the table in front of her. "Thank you," she said.

They all stood silently for a minute, looking at the pattern. Then Lina spoke softly. "Everything but the quilt itself," she said. "What happened to that quilt?"

A shadow fell across the open doorway. They all looked up. Dirk Grey was standing there.

"Hello," he said. "Coral, I saw your door was open and thought you might like a sweet roll for breakfast. I'm just taking a quick walk to the bakery."

Coral, sounding surprised and pleased, said, "How nice. But no, thank you, I've had breakfast."

Dirk nodded and turned away.

"That was thoughtful of him," said Coral. "When he first opened up his shop, he wasn't very friendly, but he's been coming around. I think he's even beginning to like quilts. He's been so much more pleasant since he quit his job at the museum and started working in his shop full-time."

"Museum!" exclaimed Jessie.

"What museum?" asked Henry at almost the same time.

Looking startled, Coral said, "The State History Museum. Why?"

"Did he work on the quilt exhibits?" Violet asked.

"Oh, no," Coral replied. "He worked in what I call the china department. But he quit last week."

Henry said, "Will you excuse us for a minute, please? We'd like to catch up with Mr. Grey. We'll be right back."

"Okay," said Lina. She was stroking the pattern as if it were an actual quilt.

As they hurried out of the shop, they heard Coral say, "So you think this was made into a wedding quilt?"

"Yes," Lina answered. "Let me tell you the story."

They didn't hear the rest. They were running down the street after Dirk Grey. They caught up with him right outside the door of the coffee shop.

"Excuse me," Jessie said breathlessly. "Excuse me, Mr. Grey?"

Dirk paused, raising his eyebrows. "Yes?" he said.

"Why did you tell us you didn't know Mr. Munsey?" Henry asked. "You worked at the museum together."

Dirk frowned. "So what if I did?"

"So you must have known him," Jessie said.

"We can ask Mr. Munsey," said Violet, "if you won't tell us."

That made Dirk Grey frown harder. "Okay," he snapped. "I know Mr. Munsey." He started to turn away.

"Why didn't you tell us the truth?" Benny asked.

The bouncy man didn't look quite so bouncy as he turned back to face them. "Because Mr. Munsey and I don't get along," he snapped. "We're not friends. We don't like each other."

"Oh," said Benny.

"Have you talked to Mr. Munsey lately?" asked Jessie.

"No," said Dirk Grey, "and if I'm lucky, I'll never have to talk to him again. We had very different ideas about what a museum should exhibit. Okay?"

He spun around and walked into the coffee shop.

The Aldens didn't try to follow.

"I think he's telling the truth now, at least

about not liking Mr. Munsey," said Violet.

"Yes," said Jessie. "And since Mr. Munsey and Mr. Grey don't like each other, it's not very likely that Mr. Munsey told him about the quilts."

"Well, I'm sure he was looking for Lina's quilts that day at the yard sale," said Violet, "even though I don't think he knows very much about them."

"It's enough that he knows they're valuable," Henry said. "Coral said he only stopped working at the museum last week. Maybe he overheard something before he left."

Jessie nodded. "Yes," she said slowly.

"Well, it's not Coral," said Violet as they walked back to the shop. "We know why she was acting so strangely when we visited her. It was because she'd just found the old quilt pattern and wasn't sure what to do."

"That leaves Dirk Grey, Regina Lott, and Mr. Munsey," said Henry.

"And the hidden treasure," Benny added.

When the Aldens entered the shop, Lina

was getting ready to leave. "Thank you again," she told Coral.

Coral nodded. "I'm glad to give you another part of your great-great-aunt's story — even if I did have to give up that quilt pattern." She picked up her quilting and waved them toward the door. "I'd better get to work on this pillow cover if I ever want to finish it," she said, and waved them out the door.

"Well, you've certainly helped me solve a mystery," said Lina.

"We have?" asked Violet.

"Yes! I know what kind of wedding quilt Aunt Hope made. I know it had lots of green in it, to match her eyes. I even have the pattern for it," said Lina. "If it weren't for you, I wouldn't have any of that."

The Aldens were glad that they had helped Lina. But they knew the biggest mystery was yet to be solved.

"Let's have some tea and cookies at my house to celebrate," Lina went on.

"Okay," said Benny promptly.

But the tea and cookies would have to wait. When they reached Lina's house, two cars were parked out front.

"That's Regina's car," said Jessie.

"And that's Mr. Munsey on the porch," said Benny.

"Regina's on the porch, too," reported Henry. "It looks like they're arguing."

The Aldens and Lina hopped out of the van and walked to the house.

"Why are you here?" Jessie blurted out.

"I drove up and saw this person snooping around the house. I thought she might be a burglar," stated Mr. Munsey. "You've told a reporter about the quilts?"

"We didn't tell her!" Benny said.

"Then who did?" demanded Mr. Munsey. "The more people who know about the quilts, the less safe it is for you to keep them in an old trunk in the attic!"

"But . . . " Benny began. He stopped when Violet squeezed his arm. He looked up and she put her finger to her lips. "Oh," said Benny. He knew Violet was reminding him that where they'd hidden the quilts was a secret.

"I'm a reporter. I find things out. It's my job," Regina said. She glanced at Lina. "And I had an appointment with Lina."

"No, you didn't," Lina said. "Not today. I told you to call first."

"So what?" Regina hissed.

Mr. Munsey said, "It's a good thing I decided to stop by here on my way home from the airport. Things are getting out of hand."

"The airport?" Jessie asked.

"I've been at a conference in Canada," said Mr. Munsey.

"When? When were you at the confer-ence, I mean?" asked Jessie.

"Since last week. I left for it a couple of hours after I came here," Mr. Munsey said impatiently.

"Did you see Dirk Grey before you left?" asked Henry.

Regina had gotten quiet and was listening intently.

"Dirk Grey! You haven't told him about the quilts, have you?" Mr. Munsey said.

"We didn't tell him, but we think he knows," said Jessie.

"Worse than telling a reporter," Mr. Munsey muttered.

Regina's face had suddenly turned red.

"Oh, dear," Mr. Munsey went on. "Dirk Grey. That spy. He must have overheard someone at the museum. Oh, dear."

"You worked at the museum, too?" Regina asked.

"I'm an expert on textiles. I specialize in quilts," said Mr. Munsey. "Oh, dear."

"You're a quilt expert?" asked Regina, holding out her microphone. "And in your expert opinion, are the quilts extremely valuable?"

That seemed to shake Mr. Munsey out of his mood. He gave Regina a cold look. He turned to Lina. "I'm going," he said. "But I'll be back."

Mr. Munsey marched to his car and drove away.

"Okay, time for my story," said Regina.

"Not now," said Lina.

Regina's sharp eyes focused on the large envelope Lina was clutching. Coral had put the quilt pattern in there for safekeeping.

"What's that? More letters?" Regina asked.

"Not now," said Lina, unlocking the door.

"But . . ." Regina said.

The Aldens followed Lina inside. Lina closed the door.

"Tomorrow," Regina shouted from the porch.

After a long wait, they heard her car drive away.

"Tea," said Lina, sounding a little tired. "And cookies."

"Yes," Benny agreed. "Cookies."

CHAPTER 9

A Quilt Trap

The Aldens sat on their front porch after dinner, talking softly. Watch was curled on a pillow, and Benny petted him as they talked.

"Mr. Munsey has been away," said Jessie. "He couldn't have tried to break into the house. And he didn't tell Dirk Grey or Regina Lott or Coral about the quilts — not unless he's a very good actor and is just fooling us."

"I don't think he is," said Violet.

"If it's not Mr. Munsey and not Coral," said Henry, "that just leaves Mr. Grey."

"He's the best suspect," said Jessie.

"Mr. Munsey thinks he could have overheard about the quilts at the museum," said Benny.

"If Dirk Grey heard about the quilts," said Henry slowly, "he must have told Coral and Regina."

Violet was nodding. "I just remembered, Regina asked Mr. Munsey if he worked at the museum, too. Who else does she know who works at the museum?"

"Or worked at the museum," said Henry. They looked at one another.

"Dirk Grey," said Jessie.

"Her face got very red when she heard his name," Violet recalled.

"She must know him. He's her source. He's the one who tipped her off about the quilts," said Jessie.

"So he's definitely the one who tried to break in?" Benny asked.

"Maybe he is, Benny," said Violet. "But why would he tell a reporter about the secret quilts he wanted to steal?"

"For that matter," Jessie added, "why was

Regina snooping around today when she knew Lina wasn't home?"

"Regina has no reason to steal the quilts," Henry said. "She just wants the story."

"Stolen quilts would be an even better story," said Jessie.

Benny was shaking his head in disbelief. "Why do so many people think old quilts are like treasure?"

They fell silent, thinking hard.

Benny kept petting Watch, who was sleepy after his big dinner.

"Watch's pillow looks sort of like a quilt," said Benny. "It's covered in patches."

No one answered. They were still thinking hard.

"You know what, Watch?" Benny said.

Watch wagged his tail just a little bit to show he was listening.

"You need a quilt of your own," said Benny, "to cover your old dog bed and keep in the stuffing. A new patchwork quilt to cover the old patchwork quilt." Benny laughed.

Violet looked up. She stared at Benny, then at Watch.

"What?" said Benny.

Violet said, "Benny . . . that might explain it!"

"Explain what?" said Henry.

"Explain where the hidden treasure is — where Hope hid her wedding quilt," Violet said.

Jessie looked up, excitement in her face. "A quilt to cover a quilt," she said.

"Like the quilt cover that Coral was making to cover the pillow," Henry said, catching on. "Hope made a new quilt and hid her wedding quilt inside!"

"She did?" said Benny.

Violet jumped to her feet. "Well, *if* she did, we've found the most valuable quilt of all, Benny," said Violet.

Now Jessie jumped to her feet. "And I think I've thought of a way to catch a quilt thief," she added.

"How?" Benny said.

"We'll need Coral's help," said Jessie. "Listen."

She told them her plan.

* * *

"Those are good stitches, Benny," Coral said. "You're really getting the hang of this." Coral was giving the Aldens a quilting lesson — and helping them set a trap to catch a thief.

Customers came into the shop as they worked, and Coral answered questions, sold sewing and quilting materials, and gave people advice. Meanwhile, the Aldens sewed and waited for their chance to act on Jessie's plan.

Then, near lunchtime, Henry glanced up at the open door of the shop and saw what he'd been waiting for. He quickly looked back down at his sewing and said, in a loud, clear voice, "I can't believe those letters had the clue to where the treasure is hidden."

"I know," said Jessie, just as loudly. "It was right there in the attic at the bottom of that trunk."

"And I'm so glad we found the wedding quilt — it's the most valuable quilt of all," added Henry.

Benny wiggled in his seat, trying not to look up or say anything that would give the trap away.

"Wait until Mr. Munsey hears about this," Violet said.

"I just hope it's safe to leave the trunk with the treasure and the wedding quilt there in Lina's attic," said Henry.

"Sure it is," said Jessie. "It's been safe there all these years, hasn't it?"

Coral had been straightening a display of thread. Now she turned to the doorway and said, "Oh! Dirk! I didn't see you standing there."

Dirk Grey stepped into the shop. "Hello," he said, bouncing slightly. "Making quilts?"

"Yes," said Benny, glad to be able to say something at last. "It's fun."

"Yes. We've even convinced Lina to try it. She's going to come over this afternoon to join us," said Henry.

"And she's bringing pizza!" Benny added.

"That's nice," said Dirk, edging out of the shop. "Well, I just wanted to say hello, Coral. See you later."

"See you later, Dirk," said Coral cheerfully.

When he was gone, Jessie let out a sigh. "I hope it works," she said.

"I hope so, too," said Henry.

"Where's the van?" Jessie said in a low voice as Lina joined them where they were waiting by the back wall of her house.

"I parked it at your house," Lina answered, "then walked back using the short-cut."

Lina and the four Aldens dashed through her backyard and in the back door of her house. Moving as quickly and quietly as possible, they hurried up the stairs to the attic.

"Good thing we didn't clean out everything for the yard sale," said Violet.

"Let's hide," Henry urged. "We may not have much time."

The five of them scattered around the attic. Jessie stepped behind an old wardrobe. Benny slid behind a chair. Violet crouched beneath a desk. Henry pulled an old blanket over him and huddled in the darkest corner of the attic. Lina hid behind an old door propped against one wall.

Then they waited.

Before long they heard footsteps moving quickly but quietly up the stairs.

Benny held his breath and hoped he wouldn't sneeze. He clamped two fingers over his nose, just in case.

The attic door swung open. Brisk, sure footsteps crossed the room. They were going straight for the trunk.

The lid of the quilt trunk creaked open. "What is this rag?" a voice muttered. "Where is the wedding quilt? And . . . "

Henry stood up. Lina stepped out from behind the door. At the same moment, Jessie, Benny, and Violet came out from their hiding places, too.

"May I help you find something?" Lina asked in a cool voice.

Regina Lott gave a small shriek as she jerked upright in surprise. She almost fell over backward. She took a few quick steps toward the door, then stopped when she saw that Henry was blocking the way.

"What — what are you doing here?" Regina stammered.

"Waiting for you," said Jessie.

"You came to steal the treasure," Benny couldn't stop himself from blurting out.

"I don't know what you're talking about!" Regina almost shouted.

"Yes, you do," Violet said quietly.

"Your source told you we'd found the treasure and that it was still in this trunk. He also told you the house would be empty this afternoon," said Henry.

"Mr. Grey," said Benny. "He told you. We let him listen to us, and he believed us!"

Regina's face turned dull red. For once, she seemed to have nothing to say.

"Mr. Grey is the one who told you about the quilts in the first place, isn't he?" said Jessie.

"He — it was just a news tip," said Regina. "We're old friends."

"A news tip — or was he trying to help you steal the quilts?" asked Violet.

"No!" gasped Regina.

"Yes," said Henry. "And this isn't the first time you've tried to take them."

Regina's face crumpled. "I just wanted to make it a better story," she explained. "Just imagine the news hook: 'Valuable Quilts Found — Then Stolen!' I would have brought them back after I'd aired the story."

"You sent Mr. Grey to look for the quilts while we were distracted with the yard sale," said Violet. "But Henry and I caught him."

Regina looked down. "That was his idea. He'd heard you might give the quilts to Mr. Munsey for the museum. Dirk hates Mr. Munsey, so he wanted to stop you."

"But he never made it to the attic," Violet finished. "He stopped to look at china along the way."

Regina nodded her head.

"He must have called you yesterday right after he saw us in the shop, getting the pattern from Coral. That's why you were here when we got back," Henry said.

"You were going to try to sneak into the

house while we were away, weren't you?" Jessie asked. "But Mr. Munsey stopped you."

"No, it wasn't like that," said Regina.

Lina spoke up. "I think it was exactly like that. You wanted a story — and a treasure. What were you going to do with the quilts?"

There was a long silence. Then Regina said quietly, "I wanted to sell them. They're worth so much money. I didn't think. I just acted. I was wrong."

"Yes, you were. So was Mr. Grey," said Benny.

Regina's shoulders slumped. "What are you going to do to me?" she asked.

Lina stared at the reporter. Then she shook her head. "Just go," she said. "You've lost your story. My quilts are safe. But if I hear of you doing anything like this again, I'm going to tell my story — about what you did — to another reporter. I hope you've learned your lesson."

Regina cast one more look at the trunk. "I'm not a very good reporter, to fall for a trick like that, am I?" she said in a dull voice. "There's no hidden treasure and no special wedding quilt, is there?"

"Time to go," said Lina, standing aside and motioning toward the attic door. "I'll show you the way out. And I'll be speaking to Mr. Grey."

Regina nodded in defeat. She walked slowly out of the attic. The Aldens listened to her plodding footsteps as she went downstairs with Lina.

A few minutes later, Lina returned. She sighed and sank onto an old stool. "The trick worked," she said. "I didn't think it would. I wonder what she thought when she saw that old hops quilt in the trunk."

Violet leaned over to lift out the old quilt. She smoothed its worn surface.

"It's not just an old hops quilt," said Violet. "Let us show you something, Lina."

CHAPTER 10

A Treasure in a Treasure

Henry helped Violet spread the hops quilt across two chairs.

Then Jessie took a tiny pair of scissors out of a carrying case in her pocket. "Coral lent me these," she explained.

She leaned over and began, very, very carefully, to cut the threads that held the outside edges of the quilt together.

"What are you doing?" Lina exclaimed.

"Watch," said Violet.

Jessie cut the seam down one side of the old quilt, then folded back the edges.

Tucked inside the hops quilt was another quilt — a beautiful, brilliantly colored quilt in a familiar pattern.

"It's the Wedding Ring quilt!" said Benny.

Lina leaped up. "Let me get another pair of scissors!" she exclaimed.

Soon they had snipped all the knots that held the two sides of the old quilt together. Those knots had held the new quilt against the old quilt, inside of it.

At last the hidden quilt was revealed.

"Oh!" said Violet. "It's even more beautiful than I thought it would be."

"And look — here's the date and your aunt's initials," Jessie pointed out.

"The same year as that last letter," Henry said.

Lina gazed at the quilt in wonder. "I don't believe it. I don't believe it," she said over and over. "Hope must have hidden it away because it was too sad for her to look at it," Violet guessed.

"But it also gave her comfort to have it near her," Henry added. "That's why the

hops quilt covering is so worn — Hope loved it to pieces."

"How did you ever figure this out?" Lina asked.

"We realized that a quilt could hide another quilt when we saw Coral making a quilted cover for a pillow," Henry explained.

"And then Benny wanted a cover for Watch's dog bed, because it is old and faded. That made me think of this old quilt, all worn and faded. And suddenly, I wondered if the worn, faded quilt could be on the outside and another quilt could be inside," Violet said.

"Look," said Benny. He pointed to the quilt. "There's an extra ring on that part."

They all looked. Sure enough, a small green ring of fabric had been patched on top of the design on one corner of the quilt.

"How strange," said Lina. "Why would Great-great-aunt Hope do that?"

Jessie reached out to touch the tiny green ring. "It's lumpy," she said.

"And hard," added Violet, squeezing the corner.

"The rest of the quilt isn't lumpy," said Benny.

Henry said, "It feels like there's something inside of it."

"The ring!" exclaimed Violet. "The green ring the color of Hope's eyes! Robert wasn't writing about the quilt after all. He meant . . ." She took the scissors and knelt down. Before anyone could say anything, she had worked three tiny stitches loose. She slid her finger under the patch. She looked up. "It's here," she said.

Now Lina knelt down, too. She carefully and delicately cut the remaining stitches that held the small green circle onto the quilt. As the last stitch came free, a gold ring with a glinting green stone fell out.

"An emerald ring!" gasped Jessie.

"Great-great-aunt Hope's engagement ring," whispered Lina. "Green like her eyes. There was a hidden treasure, after all!"

"*Two* hidden treasures!" said Benny. "The ring *and* the quilt."

"The quilt inside a quilt," said Henry.

"And the ring inside a ring," said Violet.

"A mystery inside a mystery," agreed Jessie.

"And we solved them both," said Benny.

The shop bell tinkled and Coral looked up. She beamed at the Aldens and at Lina, who stood in the doorway. "Come in, come in," she said.

"We brought a copy of the newspaper for you to see," said Benny.

"I've seen it! I've put it up on the wall!" said Coral, motioning.

On a bulletin board on one side of the shop was the article from the local newspaper. MYSTERY QUILT HOLDS HIDDEN TREASURE, the headline said, and in smaller letters, AND IS ONE, TOO, SAYS EXPERT.

"My name and my shop's name are in the article," Coral said, "for helping to solve the mystery. It's been great for business."

"How's Mr. Grey's business?" asked Lina.

"Ha! He's put a FOR SALE sign in the window," said Coral. She shook her head.

"Who could believe a nice man like that could be so sneaky? And I heard Regina Lott has taken a job in another town."

"I hope she's learned that there are better ways to get a story than trying to steal one," Henry said.

"Yes, because when she did that, she missed the biggest story of all," said Violet.

"There's going to be another story when they put the quilts on display at the museum," said Jessie. "It was nice of you to let Mr. Munsey borrow them, Lina. But I'm glad you'll be getting them back."

Lina looked down at the emerald on her hand. "It's what Great-great-aunt Hope would have wanted," she said.

"We solved the mystery," Benny said. "We've sewed this case up."

Everyone laughed. "We sure have, Benny," said Henry. "We sure have."

GERTRUDE CHANDLER WARNER discovered when she was teaching that many readers who like an exciting story could find no books that were both easy and fun to read. She decided to try to meet this need, and her first book, *The Boxcar Children*, quickly proved she had succeeded.

Miss Warner drew on her own experiences to write the mystery. As a child she spent hours watching trains go by on the tracks opposite her family home. She often dreamed about what it would be like to set up housekeeping in a caboose or freight car — the situation the Alden children find themselves in.

When Miss Warner received requests for more adventures involving Henry, Jessie, Violet, and Benny Alden, she began additional stories. In each, she chose a special setting and introduced unusual or eccentric characters who liked the unpredictable.

While the mystery element is central to each of Miss Warner's books, she never thought of them as strictly juvenile mysteries. She liked to stress the Aldens' independence and resourcefulness and their solid New England devotion to using up and making do. The Aldens go about most of their adventures with as little adult supervision as possible — something else that delights young readers.

Miss Warner lived in Putnam, Connecticut, until her death in 1979. During her lifetime, she received hundreds of letters from girls and boys telling her how much they liked her books.